HOW TO WIN A
MONSTER
RACE

For Alex — CH
For Becs xx — EE

SIMON AND SCHUSTER
First published in Great Britain in 2015 by Simon and Schuster UK Ltd
1st Floor, 222 Gray's Inn Road, London WC1X 8HB
A CBS Company

A CIP catalogue record for this book is available from the British Library upon request

ISBN: 978-0-85707-961-9
eBook ISBN: 978-0-85707-962-6

Printed in China
2 4 6 8 10 9 7 5 3 1

HOW TO WIN A MONSTER RACE

CARYL HART
& ED EAVES

SIMON AND SCHUSTER
London New York Sydney Toronto New Delhi

VROOM! VROOM!

These whizzy wheels are awesome! I've spent all morning building the track and now we're ready to race.

I'm just revving up my favourite car when . . .

"Albie!"

It's Mum.
"I need you to come and do
a job with me," she calls.
"But I'm busy!" I say.

Mum smiles. "Don't worry," she says.
"You'll like it when we get there."
We get into the car and drive to . . .

the car wash.
Excellent!
Mum puts money in the machine. But the
car wash starts before she can get back in.
UH-OH!

Slosh slosh. Swish swish.
This is really fun! But when the brushes
stop, everything looks different.
Then . . .

I am surrounded by loads of crazy-looking vehicles.
And just LOOK at the drivers! Someone shouts,
"On your marks . . . get set . . . GO!" And everyone zooms off.

paaarp!

VROOM! I think I'm in a monster race.
Mum's car roars into life and leaps forward.
It's driving ALL BY ITSELF!

Just then, a HUMUNGOUS
truck appears out of nowhere!
"Get out of my way!" roars the driver. He pushes
another car off the track and into a lake.

I screech to a stop
and leap out.
"Are you OK?" I say.
The driver sighs.
"Yes, but my race is
over thanks to that
Maxamillion in his
monster truck."
"Don't worry," I say.
"We can be a team!"

We speed away. "I'm Albie," I say.
"I'm Crystal," grins the girl monster.
We whizz around the race course, trying to catch up.
Ahead, a green car spins out of control.
"Maxamillion has sprayed gunge on the road!" shouts Crystal.
"That's cheating. We're going to skid!"

"He won't stop us that easily," I say.
I press a button on the dashboard.
"ENGAGE SUPER GRIPPERS!"
Large spikes shoot out from our tyres and
we squelch through the gunge.

The stranded driver jumps in with us and we're off!
YIPPEE!
We race around the next bend . . .

straight into a giant mound of pink jelly!
WAAAAAAHHHHH!
"NOW what are we going to do?" groans Crystal.

"It's another one of Maxamillion's tricks," I say.
"ENGAGE SUPER SQUIRTERS!"
I push another button on the dashboard.

Powerful jets of water shoot from the roof and we blast our way out.

But as we break free, our engine splutters and pops.
Uh-oh!
We need a pit stop!

"That jelly has gummed up the engine," says Crystal.
Little monsters swarm out and buzz around the car.
"Oh no," I cry. "What are they doing?"

"It's ok," laughs Crystal. "They're Sludge Slurpers."
The Sludge Slurpers clean up the car and we zoom
back into the race. **WHOOPEE!**

I drive as fast as I can. As we reach the top of a hill, we spot Maxamillion's truck.

"He's broken down," cries Crystal. "Now's our chance to overtake!"

But Maxamillion looks so miserable, I have to stop.

"I know he cheated," I say. "But it would
be mean to leave him here."
Crystal climbs out of our car.
"I suppose you're right," she sighs.

"I've been so silly," groans Maxamillion.
"I deserve to be out of the race."
"Yes, you do," smiles Crystal. "But if you're truly sorry,
you can join our team. That is, if you want to."

Maxamillion looks up. "Really?"
"Of course," I say. "Winning wouldn't be
much fun without you."

We all pile into the car.
"My turn to drive," says Crystal.
She presses the TURBO button. "Let's go!"

"You're such a good driver," gasps Maxamillion.
"Maybe next time we could be a team from the start?"
Crystal raises an eyebrow. "Only if you promise not
to cheat," she says.
Maxamillion grins. "I promise."

We speed along the final straight and whizz over the finish line. The marshal waves the chequered flag.

"We won!" shouts Maxamillion.
We all crowd onto the podium and take
turns holding the trophy.
HOORAY!

All too soon, I hear a BEEP!
Mum's car is calling me. I think it's time to go.

I head back to the car wash and say goodbye
to my new friends.
"Thanks Crystal," I grin. "I had a great time."
"Come back soon," says Crystal.

Outside, Mum is waiting.
"Oh Albie," she says. "Fancy going through the
car wash all by yourself!"
"Oh, I don't mind," I say. "It was AWESOME!"
Mum hands me a comic and we head for home.